D0291939

STERLING CHILDREN'S BOOKS
New York

An Imprint of Sterling Publishing
387 Park Avenue South
New York, NY 10016

© 2012 by Sterling Publishing Co., Inc.
Design by Jennifer Browning

ISBN 978-1-4027-8437-8

Library of Congress Cataloging-in-Publication Data Available

Distributed in Canada by Sterling Publishing
c/o Canadian Manda Group, 165 Dufferin Street
Toronto, Ontario, Canada M6K 3H6
Distributed in the United Kingdom by GMC Distribution Services
Castle Place, 166 High Street, Lewes, East Sussex, England BN7 1XU
Distributed in Australia by Capricorn Link (Australia) Pty. Ltd.
P.O. Box 704, Windsor, NSW 2756, Australia

For information about custom editions, special sales, and premium and corporate
purchases, please contact Sterling Special Sales at 800-805-5489
or specialsales@sterlingpublishing.com.

Printed in China
Lot #:
2   4   6   8   10   9   7   5   3
04/13

www.sterlingpublishing.com/kids

SILVER PENNY STORIES

The Ugly Duckling

Told by Diane Namm

Illustrated by Sarah Brannen

Once upon a time on an old farm, a mother duck sat on a nest of seven eggs.

Suddenly, six eggs hatched!

Out popped six chirpy yellow ducklings.

One egg, bigger than the rest, didn't hatch.

"Where did that egg come from?" Mother Duck wondered.

Then she heard a TOCK, TOCK, TOCK, and out popped . . .

The yellow ducklings quickly grew into pretty young ducks.

But the duckling with gray feathers wasn't pretty. He grew bigger and clumsier every day. The other ducklings didn't want to play with him.

The ugly duckling felt sad and lonely.

"Poor thing," Mother Duck said. "How could I have a duckling so different from the others?"

This made the ugly duckling feel even worse. He wept secretly every night.

Nobody loves me, he thought. *What's wrong with me?*

So one morning, he ran away from the farm.

He stopped at a pond and met
some other ducks.

"Do you know any ducklings with
gray feathers like mine?" he
asked them.

"We don't know anyone as ugly
as you," they answered.

They laughed at him and turned away.

BANG! BANG!

Feathers flew. The geese squawked and flapped their wings. The air filled with smoke.

The geese flew away.

Scared and alone, the ugly duckling hid in the willows beside the pond.

The ugly duckling was sorry he'd ever left the farm. He shivered in the willows until . . . a hand grabbed him by the neck and crammed him into a big basket!

An old woman who couldn't see very well pulled him out of the basket and tossed him into a chicken coop.

"You'd better lay plenty of eggs!" she told him as she shut the door.

A hen cackled, "If you don't lay eggs, that old woman will pop you in a pot and cook you!"

The ugly duckling didn't know what to do.

That night, the old woman forgot to close the coop door.

The ugly duckling escaped and ran as far as his webbed feet would carry him.

Soon, the ugly duckling found a bed of reeds. There was plenty of food and shelter.

"Since nobody loves me, I'll just live here by myself," he said.

So he did.

One sunrise, a flock of beautiful birds flew by. They were white with long slender necks, yellow beaks, and large wings.

"If only I could look like them," he sighed.

Then winter came. The water in the reed bed froze.

The ugly duckling wandered until he couldn't take another step. Cold and shivering, he dropped to the ground.

A kind farmer found him and put him under his arm.

"I'll take him home to my children," he said.

The farmer cared for the ugly duckling the entire winter.

By springtime, the ugly duckling had outgrown the farmer's house. So, the farmer brought him to a new home— a pond.

That's when the ugly duckling saw his reflection in the water.

Oh, my goodness. I've changed! the ugly duckling thought. *I'm not ugly, and my feathers are white.*

Just then, the flock of beautiful white birds with long slender necks returned and landed on the pond.

The ugly duckling realized that he looked just like them.

"What kind of birds are you?"
he asked.

"We're swans," they said, "and so
are you. Welcome to the flock!"

"I'm a beautiful swan," he
whispered happily.

At last he had found a home.